The JOURNEY of a BEAR HUG

written by
Kristin Barton

illustrated by
Daytona Erkan

ISBN:

UNITED HOUSE Publishing
Waterford, Michigan
info@unitedhousepublishing.com
www.unitedhousepublishing.com

Cover art and interior illustrations: Daytona Erkan
Cover and Interior formatting: Matt Russell, Marketing Image, mrussell@marketing-image.com

Published in Waterford, MI
Printed in the United States

2021—First Edition

SPECIAL SALES
Most UNITED HOUSE books are available at special quantity discounts when purchased in bulk by corporations, organizations, and special-interest groups. For information, please e-mail orders@unitedhousepublishing.com

This book is for you, dear reader, and to your
loved one who is far away and deeply missed.
May you find comfort through the words of this story.

Philip and Emilie were best friends.

They went to bear school together and

ate their bear lunches together.

They were bear neighbors who loved

to give bear hugs, but that was

before Emilie and her family moved away.

One day, Philip laid outside in the tall grass beside his home.

He watched the white, puffy clouds slowly dance past him.

There were little, yellow butterflies that skipped

from one blade of grass to another, darting past his nose.

They were happy bugs, but they didn't make him happy.

A small tear slid down Philip's cheek. He missed Emilie.

If Emilie were here, I would give her a big hug, Philip thought.

As Philip laid in the grass, watching the clouds,

he had a brilliant idea. He jumped up and ran

to the big tree at the top of the hill.

With tears in his eyes and hope in his heart,

he gave the tree the strongest bear hug he had

ever given. He squeezed and squeezed and squeezed.

All his love for Emilie was squeezed into the tree.

Tree, feeling the overwhelming love, gave a sudden shake and with a POP, Hug appeared. Hug began to climb high into Tree's branches. Tree knew the importance of her job, so she stretched out her branches as straight as they would go, reaching far into the sky.

Wind was dancing with the clouds when he looked

down and saw Tree stretching high. Wind dipped low

with a gentle breeze and swooped past the big tree.

As Wind flew past Tree, he hollered "Hello!" and saw

that Tree had a very important delivery sitting in her branches.

Wind mustered all of his strength and flew through Tree's

branches again, this time gathering the delivery into his

strong arms. This special delivery was Hug, a bear hug, and

it had a very, very long journey to make.

Hug held tight to Wind. Wind was very wild and liked to have fun. He loved to dance in the clouds and then dive to the ground, pushing over the tall grass that tickled Hug. Up and down. Wind carried Hug. They went high over frosty mountaintops that glittered in the sunlight. Then they dipped low into the valleys filled with the warm glow of the setting sun.

On through the night, Wind and Hug flew. Hug saw the moon
as it sat above the quickly approaching Ocean.

Ocean was loud. He and Wind were old friends, and
they liked to play rough. With white, foamy hands,
Ocean reached high and roared as Wind and
Hug flew above. Ocean and Wind collided, smashing into
each other with a loud laugh. Seafoam splashed
onto Hug. Hug shook off the sea spray, but
held on even tighter to Wind.

After a while, Ocean began to get sleepy and Wind

slowed down in order to not wake Ocean.

Hug was sleepy too, but tried to stay awake

by counting the stars that sparkled in the dark sky.

One star seemed to sparkle more than the others.

It's a plane, Hug realized. Wind saw it too and

glided toward it. As Wind and Hug circled the buzzing

plane, Hug looked inside the small windows. Lots of

people were inside. Some were sleeping and

others were talking and reading books.

Gradually, the dark sky filled with bright, yellow sunbeams. Morning arrived. With a quick dip to wake up Ocean, Wind sped over the water. Ocean, waking from his deep sleep, stretched tall and reached up towards Wind with a giant laugh. Ocean and Wind played and Hug held on tight.

Suddenly, Ocean hollered the loudest that Hug had ever heard. Wind and Hug were headed straight toward a giant stone wall. *Oh no,* Hug thought! *Does Wind see the giant cliff?*

As Wind and Hug swiftly raced toward the steep cliff, Wind tucked Hug close and rocketed upward. Hug gave a sigh of relief and looked down at the water. Ocean reached high with a white wave and gave one final, loud roar. Wind looked down and responded with his own loud laugh, but kept going straight up toward the blue sky.

All at once, the rock wall disappeared. Wind and Hug were suddenly soaring over a meadow where sheep were snacking on the green grass. Wind swooped low to tickle the sheep, they jumped and bleated, "Baa," in response.

Wind raced on. The grass slowly disappeared and Wind and Hug approached a city. All around were tall buildings and, far below, were cars and trucks with loud honks and clanking rattles. There were thick, brown puffs of air that Wind pushed away as he whizzed past the shiny, glass buildings. Wind was happy and whistled as he zipped past the sharp corners.

In the middle of the loud, noisy city, there was a small patch of green. Hug saw a few trees, the soft grass, and rows of colorful flowers. There were kids flying kites and a playground with swings. Wind spotted the playground too. Together, Wind and Hug slipped down the slide and Hug giggled.

Wind and Hug looked around at the green park. There was a bench beside an old tree. Wind skipped high into the sky and then slowly floated down through the tree's branches. Small birds chirped and the sun flickered brightly between the leaves of the old tree. Hug looked down and was suddenly filled with joy because sitting on the bench was a little bear, and that little bear was Emilie.

Emilie had a book on her lap, but she was looking up at the green leaves, watching them sway in the breeze. She saw the sun peeking through the branches and heard the little birds chirping. Emilie sighed. She was sad because she missed her friend, Philip. She missed playing bear games with him and she missed sharing their bear lunches. She especially missed his bear hugs.

As Emilie was looking up, she felt a gentle gust of wind encircle her and, suddenly, she felt very happy. As Hug snuggled close, Emilie felt as if Philip had just given her one of his wonderful bear hugs. Emilie smiled. She knew that no matter how far apart she and Philip were, they would always be close because of their love for each other. Suddenly, Emilie had a great idea.

Emilie jumped up and wrapped her arms around the old tree.
Emilie squeezed and squeezed. She squeezed the tree as
tight as she could, giving the biggest bear hug that that tree
had ever felt. Circling above, Wind laughed and dipped low. Hug
was waving to Wind in the branches. Hug knew exactly what to do.

THE END.

KRISTIN BARTON... As a young child, Kristin was told to dream big and she has never stopped. Today, Kristin is a speech-language pathologist and writer. She loves taking pictures, kayaking, and hanging out with family and friends. She has three dogs and a turtle. Kristin discovered Hug one night while her husband was deployed oversees. She has wanted to share this story ever since.

DAYTONA ERKAN... Hello! I am Daytona, a daughter, sister, wife, mama, friend, and artist. I have always loved to paint. It helps me communicate what's in my head or heart that I have a tough time expressing in words. As an Army child, that frequently moved growing up. I had to say goodbye to several friends. I would have loved to send them a big bear hug! This book means the world to me, and I am so grateful to illustrate Hug's journey.

CPSIA information can be obtained
at www.ICGtesting.com
Printed in the USA
LVRC090104011221
704951LV00003B/65